Total Blueprint
FOR WORLD
DOMINATION

Jolene Stockman

ISBN-13: 978-1466359307
ISBN-10: 1466359307

CONTENTS

"You've got one life, one shot, and all the power to make it happen. Get ready to dream big and live big. It's all up to you. And it starts now."

Total Blueprint for World Domination is a powerful life-planning book for teens that will inspire.

This book lets readers:
*Explore hidden passions and find direction.
*Create heart-pounding, toe-tingling goals.
*Recruit an army for support.
*Design a dream world and make it happen.
*Achieve world domination step-by-step.

Full of tips and tricks for tackling life's challenges, Total Blueprint for World Domination is a book that will motivate readers to take their life to the next level.

"Anything is possible. And anything is possible for you. Believe it. Total Blueprint for World Domination takes you from this very second to your greatest dreams. So, are you ready?"

www.jolenestockman.com

* * * * *

Light Bulb: Drive Through

The world needs its ass kicked. You're going to do it.
The worlds awaiting you are bright and varied.
Target, aim, fire!

* * * * *

You've heard it all. They say; "no," they say; "you can't," they say; "you have to." Whoever they are and whatever they say, they're wrong. Actually, only you know what's right for you. They can talk all they want but this is your life, your world, and you call the shots.

You're about to pull up at the great big drive through window of life, and place your order. Your life. It's a big one. Not many people know exactly what they want. There are some easy options. There are some scary ones. You could drive straight through, and get someone else's order.

But every action will be a choice. And if you don't ask, you won't get. You don't ask? You can't get.

We have never been in a more fantastic world; where teenagers get online and start million dollar companies, where octogenarians go to college for the first time. So, when you order? Be specific, be sure, and be ready! You have the potential to be, do or have anything (and everything) you want. Why not? Better yet, what if?

For world domination you need two things: a superhero and a blueprint. You've already sorted the hero (they're wearing your shoes), and as you work through this book you will create a total blueprint for domination of your world. Oh, and when you hear "world domination," forget weapons and wars. Think: magical and emotional worlds. Think: your reality. Achieving world domination means empowering yourself to create the world you want.

Scene One: Super You. We're going to create a personal vision. This vision will set the foundation for your new world. Plus, you'll find out why you are the best person to make your dreams come true!

Scene Two: World Domination. We're going to dig up the things that get you excited, and find ways to bring them into your life. We'll define and design exactly where you want to go. And we'll dream: big, bigger, biggest, and mind-blowing!

Scene Three: Target. We'll get SMART, and set up your targets. You'll feel the deliciousness of anticipation. Your perfect world is well within your sights!

Scene Four: Aim. This is it! We're going to take your dreams, and set up a plan. We will aim for your perfect world. Aim for it, ready to take over!

Scene Five: Learn. We'll get to know the coolest person on the planet - you! When you ask for help, the universe opens up. You'll get ready to create your world, and find out how learning can turn any situation into success!

Scene Six: Expose Yourself. You will figure out your challenges, and dig up more of the truth about you. You'll get even braver, and learn how to handle the three kinds of fear: brain, heart, and kryptonite.

Scene Seven: Get to the Yes. You only have control over one person. But you are not on your own! Recruit your world domination army. Plus - persistence, enthusiasm, desire: we'll find ways to get to the yes!

Scene Eight: Fire! As you take over your world, you will start to feel the power that you were born with. Your life is an incredible force. You can change, create, grow, inspire. It's all up to you! What are your intentions?

Scene Nine: Let Go. You will let go of your beautiful plans and detailed goals. You will relax, have faith, and know that you are open to the ultimate possibilities.

The world domination symbol is throughout this book. This is where you'll find tools and jewels you can use to design (and dominate!) your dream world.

The world needs its ass kicked. You're going to do it. It starts now!

Scene 1: Super You

When was the last time you were seriously happy? Not the Everything-is-Perfect kind of happy, but the Just-Totally-in-the-Moment-Light-and-at-Peace kind. When you are happy, your brain relaxes, your heart glows, and your world flows more easily. And you know what? You deserve to be happy more. You really do. Not just because you are awesome (because you are), but because the great big drive through window of life comes complete with as much happiness as you can order. Happiness is part of the deal!

We're here to get you exactly what you want. World domination. Why not? You have the potential to dominate your world, and experience incredible happiness, starting now! We're going to get really selfish here and just talk about you! Only you know the infinite details of your world. Only you know the trap doors and the secret rooms, only you know where the treasures are kept. Your mission is happiness over your lifetime, and you have control of that every second!

You are the most important person in your world, and the person you have all the power over. The trick? To know when to be you, and when to be Super You. Like that Christmas cracker joke; what's the difference between a combo and a super combo? Super Combo has a cape. When you drape yourself in the cover of confidence - and it doesn't have to be a physical cape or tights (but if you'd feel more comfortable, go for it!) you become your best self. So, what's the difference between you and Super You? Cloaking yourself in a feeling of power and purpose, having a plan, and knowing that you're the best person to carry it out.

Every superhero has a purpose. Whether it's stopping crime or seeking treasure, they all have a reason to leap out of bed in the morning. Now's the time to discover yours! A personal vision reflects who you are, and who you want to be.

Think about Lady Gaga, Jamie Oliver, and Robert Rodriguez. These people have strong personal visions. Their vision gives them clarity, and this clarity gives them confidence, style, and a purpose. Maybe you don't know what you want yet – that's okay. Just know that if and when you want to find out, the tools are ready!

A personal vision is a statement about your goals, dreams and values. Businesses and other organizations call this a mission statement. Your personal vision can start with a dream for your world: who you would be, and what you would do if there was nothing in your way (because you know, there really is nothing in your way!) Wait, so what's a dream? A dream is the biggest and best you can imagine for your life. A dream has no limits! That's the best place to start. After that, a personal vision brings your dreams into everyday life.

Scary? Exciting? Definitely! Why do we keep so many things in our lives that make us feel less than perfect? (And what if that's possible? That no matter how much things can suck, we're here for a reason and that getting through the crap will give us the tools we need to achieve it? If you knew that this is the absolute truth, would it change how you see yourself?)

Deep breath.

You've got one life, one world, and one person to get a hold of. I love the story of the pirate captain and his lucky shirt (stop me if you've heard this one). Long ago, when sailing ships ruled the waves, a captain and his crew were being attacked by another pirate ship. The crew were freaking out, so the captain called out to the first mate, "Bring me my red shirt!" He put on his red shirt and they fought off the pirates, with only a few getting sliced and diced.

Later that night, a new guy got brave, and asked the captain, "What's up with your red shirt? Why do you wear it into fights?" The captain told him, "If I'm wearing a red shirt and I get cut, the blood won't show. You guys will think I'm okay, and keep fighting." Smart thinking. The next morning, the lookout screamed. Pirate ships were all around, loading cannons and preparing to attack. "Bring me my red shirt!" called the captain, "and my brown pants."

In your world, you're the captain, the master, the head honcho, the big cheese. You are the ring leader, the director, and your job is to captain the ship of your life. Your crew are your pounding heart and shaking hands, your knotted stomach and swirling head. And you lead the way with a plan. There are days that you'll do things because you believe in yourself, and then there are days when you'll pull out your red shirt and your brown pants.

And remember, Superman isn't Superman all of the time – just when he needs to be. It's okay to Clark Kent your way through the day. Even Wolverine retracts his claws! Just know that you can be Super You whenever you want! You can put on your superhero persona, become Super You, rescue some kids / stand up for yourself / give a speech / fight a villain, and when it's all over, try to remember which phone box you left your pants in.

Super You is who you become when you are your very best self. By creating and writing down your own personal vision, you will have a tool to stay inspired!

Your Personal Vision

Start by thinking about what makes you Super You. What makes you special, what makes you *you*? Ask:

- What am I good at?
- What do I feel strongly about?
- What do I like doing?
- What makes me special?
- What are my passions?
- What do I want to do with my life?
   (If you don't know the answers yet, focus on how you want to feel in your world: happy? Excited? Peaceful?)

Your personal vision can be as simple as Nike's: "Just do it!" or as meaty as the Declaration of Independence. Because your personal vision is just that - personal. Keep an open mind, but know that your personal vision only has to be true for you. It doesn't have to look or sound a certain way. It doesn't have to impress anyone. It only has to make you feel good!

If the idea of a personal vision doesn't feel right to you, you could think about creating a metaphor for your life. The word "metaphor" comes from the Latin word "metaphora," meaning "to transfer." So, a metaphor takes the elements of one thing and applies them to something else. For example:
- "She has a fiery temper." Her fury may be scorching, but she isn't actually on fire!
- "Life is a rollercoaster." Life is an exciting ride, but you can do it outside of Disneyland!

For your blueprint, you can choose an image or symbol that represents who you are or who you want to be. You can create a metaphor for your life. Here are some examples:

- You may see yourself as a race car: powerful, motivated, and navigating through life heading for awesome prizes.

- Or maybe you're a sun: bright and happy, spreading light wherever you go.

- You could be a chef in the kitchen of life: mixing exotic ingredients to create amazing adventures.

(My metaphor is lighting fireworks; I want to spark the fuse in others! I want to inspire and motivate people to aim for the stars and dominate their world!)

You can see how a metaphor can not only give you positive words to use; it can give you an image as well. You can use this image to instantly feel strong, happy and purposeful!

Once you have a personal vision or a metaphor for your life, you can access your magic whenever you want. The world is at your fingertips, and your power is also your choice. For you, world domination and blueprint design is just the beginning. Your life is in the everyday, what you do while your plans bubble away. Love your life. Believe that it was designed for you. Believe that every person, situation, and element around you has been hand-picked to allow you to get the most out of this world.

And if you don't love your life? Change it. Don't accept anything that doesn't make you glow with pride that it's yours. Love everything you eat, wear, think and do. And if you can't love it outright, love where it'll take you. If there are things in your world that don't make you feel smiley - get them out! We're accepting far too much crap from a world where anything is possible.

The way to happiness is by filling your life with the things that you love. Big things – like friends, a kick-ass career, or (and!) a peaceful family life. And little things – like comfy clothes, or a jam-packed Ipod. Happiness is found in the everyday; it's chocolate, sunshine, puppies. Really. You can see the crap in life, or you can see the cool. Happiness is a choice in every moment and you are in charge of that choice.

This is exciting! It means you don't have to wait for anyone to give you permission to be happy; you can start creating the the life you want right now! You can take all the actions, you can have all the feelings, and you can make all the decisions.

We're here to work on your total plan for world domination, and it starts from a place of exquisite anticipation. Total belief that anything is possible – and that anything is possible for you. Know that all the achievement and success in the world can't replace a deep passion for the life you have. We're going to get you feeling that with all your heart! Both you, and Super You.

Raise your expectations, and the world will meet them.

Super You

What makes you Super You?
How do you want to feel in your world?
What is your personal vision?
What is the metaphor for your life?

Once you have a personal vision or a metaphor for your life, you can access your magic whenever you want. Use them to feel instantly strong, happy and purposeful!

Scene 2: World Domination

"Whatever you can do, or dream you can, begin it.
Boldness has genius, power, and magic in it."
Johann Wolfgang von Goethe

* * * * *

We all have the potential to uncover our passion, tackle the why-nots, and live out our dreams. So, why isn't everyone doing it? Here's the secret: a perfect world doesn't exist. There are millions of them. World domination means conquering the space around you, finding happiness in your everyday. Because there is no real world, just the one you create.

Identify the world you wish to dominate, your perfect world, the ultimate life for you. You don't have to have everything, just everything you want. And you don't have to do everything, just everything that excites you. Life is a drive through, a kitchen with limitless ingredients. We all have different dreams and different worlds we want to dominate. Your favorite food is someone else's phobia.

Your dream job is someone else's worst nightmare. Your perfect world is unique to you.

What will make the difference? Having a plan. Just like the Trojan War. The Trojan War dragged on for years. The Greeks couldn't break into Troy and the Trojans couldn't scare them off. Everyone had a goal; everyone was clear on what it was that needed to be done. The Greeks wanted in, and the Trojans wanted them gone. But still the war dragged on. Being on the right track is not enough. Knowing what you want is not enough. People say that even if you're on the right track, you'll get run over if you just sit there. You have to have a plan, you have to act. Back in Troy there were plenty of ideas, but what was needed was a sequence of ideas, aiming for a goal, set into action. A plan. Odysseus didn't just have an idea, Odysseus had a plan. And so, under the cover of darkness and a wooden horse, the Greeks stormed Troy, and the war ended.

Everyone is looking up at their own Trojan walls, and figuring if they wait long enough it will be time, fate will do her bit, and problem solved. Never mind the people on the other side, looking up at the same walls, and praying to the same fates. Meanwhile ten years go by, and no one can remember what the point of all this was, or what exactly they wanted from the other side anyway. So, here's the deal: world domination means taking fate into your own hands, it means looking up at the walls that challenge you, and figuring out a way to get to the top.

It's up to you. What are your goals for your life? Think big. Your blueprint can cover every area. Ooh, and if you want a digital one, go to: totalblueprint.com/myworld.html

Start by looking at your world from space. From there, you can see that your world is made up of lots of different areas. Like:

* Relationships - friends, family, partner, other.
* Professional - education, career, image.
* Spiritual - self-development, beliefs, religion.
* Abundance - love, money, stuff.

Once you've figured out the different areas that make up your world (and hey, right now there might only be one!) write them down. Only you can decide what your perfect world looks like, and no one has to know what you include – or what you leave out.

Your perfect world is powered by passion. An overwhelmingly positive feeling of joy and purpose in your life. When you uncover your passion you'll know. The thought of it will fill you with energy, warmth and happiness. It will give you a sense of purpose and drive!

Passions can be absolutely specific ("I want to be a neo-natal surgeon by day and a party planner by night!") or totally general ("I want to work with furry animals!") For some people, it takes a lifetime of exploring and adventures to nail down their passion, and for some people it may change all the time. You may have one passion when you're ten, and another when you're twenty – or a different passion every week! You may have one passion that radiates through your entire world ("I love music!") or feel different passions in each area ("I love being a good sister, I love being rich, I love purple!") The main thing is to start looking for those feelings of pure, positive, passion. Find the things that light you up. Why not fill your world with joy? Why not seek happiness? You only get one shot! So live your life!

And while you're looking for happiness, feel the difference between wanting something to fill a hole inside you, and wanting something because you love it. Loving something lights you up inside, but some holes can never be filled. Ask yourself, why is this my passion? And (especially!) how does it make me feel? For some people, their heart is their guide. For others, it's an adrenalin jolt, a brain quiver, or an irresistible pull. But however it shows up for you, it will feel good, and like nothing else you have experienced!

To uncover your passion, we're going to jump into a Brain Dig! A Brain Dig is an adventure. A treasure hunt. A journey to the joy inside you. First up, relax. There's no pressure. This is totally for you. Let your mind go. Dream. Run free. At this stage, possibilities are rampant. You have the power to design your destiny, and to create your perfect world. And like in fashion, movies, and buildings, it all happens on paper first!

Brain Dig

1. Daydream! Imagine all the things you want to be, do, have, or experience in your world.
2. Get a corkboard or scrapbook. Or open up a document or webpage.
3. Find words and images that represent who you are, and who you want to be.

You can do this whatever way feels right for you. Write in a journal, make lists, cut up magazines, take photos, Google search, start a blog, or make a video. Start getting an idea of how you want your world to look. Don't make any choices, no decisions are necessary. Don't judge your dreams, just want them! Find the things that make your heart pound, then jump right in! And why do this? Because when it comes down to it, we all want the same thing – happiness. And the way to happiness is by filling your life with the things that you love.

Bonus: look around you. Look at the physical things that surround you in your life now – the posters on your walls, the piles of things you wake up seeing, the books you read. Look at the clothes you wear, and the things you own. Touch them, and feel their effect on you. Do you love them? Do they make you feel good?

When you're digging around in your head looking for the things that give you that wicked feeling (the feeling that with that job / book / friend or shirt, your world is complete), know that digging out what you love can mean getting dirty. This is because sometimes the things that make us the happiest are the secret dreams: the art project you're scared people will judge you for, the 57 Chevy that you're saving up to buy. Maybe what really gets you going is dancing or numbers, painting or texting – but figuring it out is the first step. Maybe what you're looking for is something deep, dark and forgotten about. Something you pushed down or tucked away.

Like school subjects. You love art, even though you go crazy trying to get the bottle looking even on both sides, so what do you do? You drop art, and pick up accounting. You do it because you know you can get higher marks with accounting. Because that's the sensible choice, it will make your parents happy, help get you a good job, stability. And that's why we have to get dirty here! Following your happiness may not be the easy, sensible path. Your true passion may be that thing you loved when you were five. You might have stopped making cardboard robots to take to school because the teacher wouldn't let them sit at your desk. Think back. You make the decisions here; it's not about what you're good at or what makes anyone else happy. This is your life and your world (and I'm sure once I got the tinfoil antennae and milk bottle cap eyes working, those robots would have really helped out against the school bullies!)

You need to know what makes you tick, and why you do what you do. No one knows you better than you, and your treasure is ready to find!

Your World

So, how do you dig out a buried passion? Start hunting for things that really resonate with you, things that pull you. Anything. Events, products, careers, colors or words. Focus on one and develop your thoughts: what does it mean to you? How could you grow it? Bring it into your life? How would your life be with more of that in it? Write it all down, chat with a friend, or to yourself. Go all out! You are an expert in the subject – you.

Think about how much you love chocolate or your pet. Figure out the things that fill you up, make you zing. Go back to the areas of your perfect world:

* Relationships - friends, family, partner, other.
* Professional - education, career, image.
* Spiritual - self-development, beliefs, religion.
* Abundance - love, money, stuff.
* Bonus! Use whatever works for you.

You can use these areas to focus your Brain Dig. What makes you happy in your relationships? At home or in school? What makes your world shiny, exciting, and full of possibilities? Once you have started designing your perfect world, the universe will start sending more: more signs, more jewels, more for you to add. Your perfect world is always changing, because you are always changing, too! And as you get more specific, you can imagine each area of your world lighting up.

This is the part where anything is possible! Go big. Super-big. Enjoy singing? Cut a demo! Love crocodiles? Build a wildlife park! If it makes you feel good, it is your path. Aim high! Look for joy! There are a million worlds, and they are all open to you. We're not just ordering the chance to play sports for a living; we're ordering a gold medal for swimming at the next Olympic Games. We're not just ordering a trip to San Diego Zoo, we're ordering a global tour of animal sanctuaries. Think bigger. And biggest! And do it totally pure. Right now don't think about hows or why-nots, don't let yourself worry about whether you can or who-do-you-think-you-are. Bits of your heart and brain store your future plans. This is about telling those parts of you that you expect success! And you expect it big!

Ooh, do you feel it? The adventure? The potential? You've kicked it off! Now, you're ready to set some kick-ass goals!

World Domination

Do a Brain Dig!
Define and design the ultimate life for you.

What do you love?
What does your perfect world look like?

*Achieving world domination means empowering yourself
to create the world you want. It means conquering the
space around you, finding happiness in your everyday.*

Scene 3: Target

"Success is getting what you want,
but happiness is wanting what you get!"
Dale Carnegie

Batman wants to clean up Gotham City. Superman wants to protect mankind. Shrek wants to live happily ever after. What do you want?

Your goals describe what you want, and where you're going. They can be a simple sentence, or more detailed. But they are the building blocks of creating your perfect world.

You've been on a Brain Dig. You've started imagining your perfect world, filled with all the things that make you feel good. Now it's time to make it real!

We're going to get specific. We're going to make it happen! Your goals can grow with you, so just make them perfect for you right now. You can have goals for every area of your world, or start with just one – it's all up to you. You can always change them. Dream, explore, and have fun! Because now it's time to hone in on exactly what you want for your world!

Next Steps

Here's the Plan...
You've used your Brain Dig to identify your passions. Next we're going to:

1. Expand your perfect world out even further.
2. Dream big for every area of your life!
3. Target your favorite areas, ready to set some goals.
4. Get SMART!

You've divided your perfect world into lots of different areas, and you've started finding all the things that make you happy. Now, we can start expanding. For each area, ask yourself: what are all the things I want to have? Want to learn? Want to see? Want to do? You can jump into all of the areas at once, or one at a time. Whatever works for you.

If you want, you could write them out like a menu:

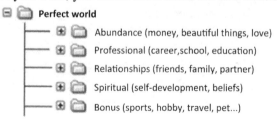

You can see that your areas can be expanded by listing the things you want to see, feel, have, or experience. For example:
- Abundance: To see beautiful things, to feel love, to have heaps of money.

If you want, you can expand them even more, like this:

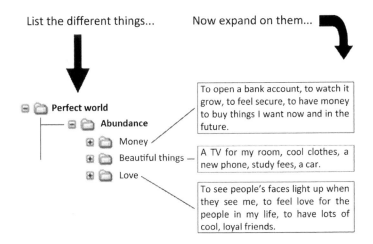

This part's AWESOME! Think big, dream huge, and do it because it feels great! Think of all the things that get you excited. Do they make your heart race? Pound? Or just flutter? Think bigger. What if you could do, be or have *anything*?

Now you're ready to start making it happen! Pick an area of your life that you want to see sparkle. Scan the areas below, or the areas you have created. See if one jumps out:

* Relationships - friends, family, partner, other.
* Professional - education, career, image.
* Spiritual - self-development, beliefs, religion.
* Abundance - love, money, stuff.
* Bonus! Use whatever works for you.

You can set goals for all of your areas, or one at a time. You could even pick one area a month, or leave them until you feel inspired. It's your world, your choice! You don't have to know it all right now. You have your whole life to figure it out! Everything is happening perfectly.

When setting goals, the trick is to get super specific. Have you heard of SMART? It's a goal setting guide that might help. It stands for: Specific, Measureable, Attainable, Realistic, and Time-Bound. Let's take a closer look!

Specific: Being specific means paying attention to detail. This is where you define your goal exactly. To get specific, think about how your goal looks, feels, sounds, smells, tastes! For example: "I want to be successful!" is general. If this is one of your goals, think about what what success means for you. Is it being happy in each moment? Having a job you love, or achieving a qualification? A more specific goal would be: "I want to grow my own vegetables and eat them!" This goal outlines exactly what you want to do, it is specific.

Measureable: If your goal is measurable, you will know when you've achieved it. For example: "I want to be rich!" is tricky to pin down. To make a goal measureable, think about how you will know when you've achieved it. So, for this example: what does being rich mean to you? Is it spending time with friends? Buying a car? Having a million dollars? A more measureable goal would be: "I want to save $100 a month!" If you set this goal, you will be able to measure when you have achieved it.

Time-Bound: By adding when you are going to do something, it makes it real! Add a deadline, and commit to a date. This will help motivate you into action. For example: it doesn't sound very urgent to say, "I am going to get fit." Try instead: "I am going to train for, and enter the May 2016 City to Mountain Relay." Can you feel how much more exciting this goal is? Being Time-Bound gets you fired up!

Achievable: This means that your goal can be completed. Because while everything is definitely doable, not everything is under your control. For example: "I want to marry Justin Bieber!" Okay, how doable is this? Apparently, when Katie Holmes was a teenager she said in an interview that she wanted to marry Tom Cruise. And whether it was her goal or fate, she did it. Everything is possible. But the deliciousness of a goal is being able to take action towards it. When setting your goals, focus on your actions and intentions, no-one else's. Make your goals achievable, by making them yours! Maybe instead, the goal could be: "I want to open my heart and be a loving person."

Realistic: A goal that is realistic for one person might be more challenging for someone else. For example: "I'm going to read a book a week for a year, and review them all on my blog." For a fast reader, this goal might be perfect. For someone else, maybe not. Consider how much you're taking on. Ask yourself: am I physically, mentally, emotionally able to achieve my goal? Maybe instead, the example goal could be: "I'll read a book every month for a year and review my four favorites on the blog." Make your goals challenging, but possible! Only you know what is realistic for you. Only you get to decide what is possible. Don't let anyone tell you that you can't!

There are heaps of goal setting tools online. If the SMART guidelines work for you, use them. Use anything that makes the process fun, and ignore anything that doesn't feel good to you. Your goals are your business, and they only need to matter to you. Plus, setting them doesn't have to be the end. Set a goal, and when you achieve it – set another one! Every goal can help you make your life even more amazing!

Target

Jump into your blueprint and set some exciting goals!
- What areas are in your perfect world?
- What do you want for your life?
- What is the biggest you can dream for your world?
- What are your goals?

Once you have set some delicious goals, we're going to make them a reality!

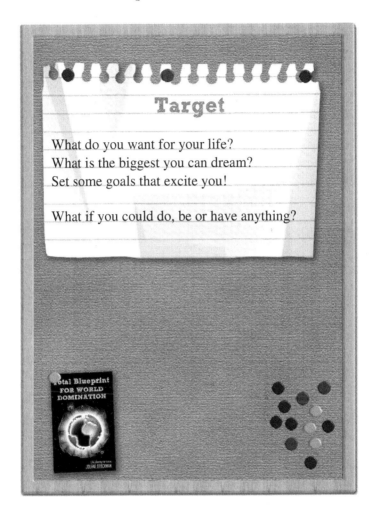

Target

What do you want for your life?
What is the biggest you can dream?
Set some goals that excite you!

What if you could do, be or have anything?

Your goals grow with you,
so make them perfect for you right now.
You can always change them.
Everything is happening perfectly.

* * * * *

Scene 4: Aim

* * * * *

Here it is. This scene brings your dream into reality – on paper at least! It sets you up with the ultimate to-do list. The path that once complete will launch you into your new world. Head into this section with a bubbling determination! This is your path to perfect happiness! Anything you want can be achieved, and you have the power to make it happen. Take a deep breath – the first step is a dizzying place to be!

Warning! Don't forget the importance of identifying and targeting exactly what you want. A full-on blueprint is no good if it dominates the wrong world! So, only complete this part if your Brain Dig from Scene 2 makes your heart pound, and your goals from Scene 3 make your feet tingle to go out and just start!

You've started digging for the things that make life worth living for you. Check out your blueprint. You've uncovered your passion, set your sights on specific areas, and decided to take over the world, now what?

Take the guff from your Brain Dig, and picture yourself in your perfect world. Imagine yourself exactly where you want to be - and I mean big, as big as it gets. This is the day you achieve your goal. The moment that the dream is your reality. Think: Joy, Peace, Oscar, Gold Medal, Degree with Honors, One Hundred Million Dollars... (And if you're not sure where you want to be? Reread your personal vision, go on another Brain Dig, and have fun exploring your passions!)

The trouble with thinking big is that it starts to look hazy. Unrealistic. Mythological. So, this part of the blueprint brings it in to focus. When I think about writing a book or a script that changes the world for someone else, I get that heart pounding, big-eyed, puppy-spirit feeling. If you love movies, then maybe to you the coolest, most exciting thing that represents success would be a gold popcorn for best movie – an MTV Movie Award. "I want an MTV Movie Award!"

Whoa – road block! Who am I to think I can get an MTV Movie Award? Or a gold medal? Or to even think about the thing that important / special / lucky / beautiful people do? Newsflash: you are Walt Disney before he met the mouse. You are Oprah before the talk show, Jamie Oliver before food. But better than all of that – you are you! You are the only one of you that exists, and you are on the brink of becoming who you were always meant to be. You are one decision away. Don't let that whiny little voice in your head fill you with crap that'll stop you swooping down the bat pole, and making a difference! You are already exactly where you need to be, and everything you dream of is waiting for you to go out and grab it! This is your world, and you are the star. In this moment, no one is watching, and in this moment your dreams are yours. Doubting yourself is not an option. Don't if or but – just dream.

There's a part of you, way inside, that never changes. It just waits to be more of itself. And that little shiny glow believes in you and tingles when you start thinking about how you want your world to be. That's the part we're talking to here. Block out the bad, and snuggle up to the glow. And when you're there, get cozy. Yes! You want an MTV award, a Nobel Prize, and your own business. Yes! You want a gold medal, a scholarship, and true love. Yes! You want to aim high, live your dreams, and dominate your world. Yes! Yes! Yes!

Okay, so now what? Kick your imagination into gear. Picture yourself in the future that's waiting for you. They're putting the medal around your neck, you're cashing the check or holding the diploma, you're accepting your golden popcorn. Now think, what was the very last thing you had to do to be in that moment?

...To get an MTV Award you have to be nominated.

Play it again. So you've been nominated. Imagine the feeling of being nominated (or qualifying for the Olympics, or completing the final paper, etc.) Think, what was the very last thing you had to do to be in that moment?

...To be nominated for an MTV Movie Award, you have to have made a movie.

And what would you have to do to be there?

...To make a movie, you have to have a kick-ass script, and know how to tell a story well.

Work your way back. Write out the steps. Some will need a bunch of different levels under them. If you need to, do this on a huge piece of paper. Don't limit yourself! And definitely don't limit yourself because your paper isn't big enough. There will always be more paper, but only ever one you! Write the steps out whatever way feels right: a list, a chart, a mind map, a tree diagram. It might even look like a big scribbled mess, but that's okay, because only you need to read it!

Let's keep going with that MTV Award:

...To have a script, you need to write one, or collaborate with a scriptwriter...To know how to tell a story well, you have to study film...To tell a story, you have to have life experience...To get life experience? Live life, take risks and take note!...To be able to tell a story well, you have to study writing and have experience...To tell a story well, you need to study writing.

When you accept your potential, and begin to dream as big as you can, ideas will begin to rattle around. Big and crazy, or small and bizarre. Ask all of these ideas two questions: does it make me happy? If it does it stays. Then ask: why not?

...An MTV award. Why not?
...Because I haven't been nominated. Why not?
...Because I haven't made a movie. Why not?
...Because I haven't written a script.

Ask after every level. The answer to "Why not?" becomes your to-do list.

...I can't get an MTV movie award. Why not? Because I haven't made a movie. So, make a movie...I can't make a movie. Why not? I don't have a production company, and the resources that go with it. So, start your own business...I can't start my own business. Why not? I wouldn't know where to start. So, go on a business course, or intern with a production company.

Tackling why-nots solves problems, and opens up possibilities. Hack at the why-nots until only the dream remains.

Once you know where you're heading, it can all become simple. Everything is possible. (And if you don't see a way, get together a roomful of extra brains to help you figure it out! We'll talk about this more in Scene 7, when we recruit your army!) So, this is your plan. You want to take over the world? Cool! Just start now! Act now!

Einstein said: *"A body at rest remains at rest unless acted upon by an external force."*

Don't let that external force be the force of someone else's plan. Take charge! Create your own plan, and act on it! Go through the steps of your plan. Ask yourself: what would someone need to do or have to get that? And write the answer underneath. At times it may splinter into several paths. Push on. Write it all down.
Turn your "Why not?" into "What if?"
...What if you give it a go and it helps you find your way?
...What if you take a chance and it turns out to be amazing?
...What if everything works out beautifully?

You now have a kind of outline, a list of all the things you need to do to get where you want to be. Take this list, and pull it apart some more: what resources do you already have for each step? What tools or contacts do you need? How can you get them?

Take the lower levels lower and lower, until something freaky happens...
- To study writing and film, I will need to do assignments.
- To do assignments, I need to enroll in a class.
- To enroll in a course, I need to research all available classes, and select one.
- To research courses, I can go online now.
...suddenly you hit something that you can do now. Right now.

It's pretty amazing when you realize that you can put your foot on the path to exactly what you want this second. That when you open that book or go online today, you are carving out a direct link to your perfect world.

Catch your breath. Is your heart racing? Is your blood pumping? That is not your knees knocking, it's opportunity! So, don't stop there! Go up through the levels and work out when you can complete each step.

5 years from now.
4 ½ years from now.
4 years from now.
Complete over 3 years.
Begin next year.
This year.
2 weeks from now.
Today!!!

You now have a timeline. Put the actual dates on it, and drink in how doable this is! Feel the incredible deliciousness of being able to do something right now.

This is your step-by-step plan. Keep a copy somewhere special, and create a simplified version to use every day. Write out your destination, and the big steps that take you there. Then post it where you can relish it: your diary, your wallet, your car, your bathroom, and school folder. Everywhere! Picture your success, and cultivate an unstoppable desire! (I have a special hardcover notebook that inspires me when I see it.)

The Plan

1. What does success look like for this goal, or this area of your life? Is it a party? A car? A qualification? A feeling?

2. Use your imagination, and picture yourself there. Put yourself into your amazing future.

3. What was the last thing you had to do to be in that moment? Write it down. Then ask, what was the last thing you had to do to be in this new moment?

4. Work your way back, writing everything down.

5. For each step, ask yourself: "Does that make me happy?"
- If it doesn't, either find another way to achieve it, or find a way to get excited about the step.
- If it does, ask, "Then why haven't I done this step yet? Why not?" The answer becomes your to-do list!

6. What do you need to do or get for each step or level?

7. Keep going back until you hit something that you can do now. Right now!

8. Add a timeline – this is doable!

9. Simplify your list, and post it everywhere. You are on your way!

You have the dream, the vision, and the plan. Savor successes, and enjoy each step. Every time you hit a target, congratulate yourself. You are closer and closer. The key now is action. Take a little action every day that pulls you towards the next step. And be open to making changes. At some point a career goal may collide with a friendship goal. Be flexible. Flow where life takes you. Your blueprint is a plan that takes you from this very moment to your dream. And even dreams can change. Your life can be spun around in a flash. Be ready to switch plans if your heart pulls you somewhere else. You know what? Your happy ending changes all the time! Something in life may grab you in a new way. Be open to the universe giving you a hint, a nudge, or a shove. This is all about you.

Aim

Imagine yourself in your perfect world.
Write out the steps.
Does it make you happy?

Simplify your list – post it everywhere!

*Your blueprint is a plan that takes you from
this very moment to your dream. Be flexible.
Your happy ending changes all the time!*

* * * * *

Scene 5: Learn

Non scholae, sed vitae discimus.
"We don't learn from school but from life."

Nosce te ipsum!
"Know thyself!"

* * * * *

Life is a big, delicious, learning journey. Even when you're not at school, you're always learning. And you know what? You're always teaching, too! Because it's not about the weird math stuff you're sure you'll never use, or the Latin vocab you memorize to pass the test. Your life is made up of a zillion experiences. And the awesome-creepy-cool thing? If you don't learn something in life, it keeps coming back until you do.

Start with you! You are the hero of your movie. You are the captain of your ship. No one knows you better than you. If something is getting in the way of what you want, it's time to take charge! Let's jump in and figure out what makes you tick!

Do you put things off? Important things? Things that you just can't make yourself do? This is a big one, the arch nemesis of world domination: procrastination. When you put off studying for a test, completing a project, or going out and pushing your boundaries, there are consequences. Sure, you dissolve your fear and feed your boredom, but you also kill opportunities, and delay your world takeover!

Let's tackle it head on! Find ways to drop the excuses. Do it, and do it now! Here we go, procrastination:

1. Admit it. Do you put things off? Do you do it regularly? On purpose? Think about a recent example. And it doesn't have to be big. Maybe you still haven't cleaned out that top drawer, even after promising yourself a thousand times.

2. Think about what you might get out of putting that thing off. And don't lie! This is just for you. Dig up your reasons. And then, when you think you've got it, dig a little more! Here are some examples:

"I do my best work last minute and under pressure!"

"I like to keep stress to a minimum by leaving things. I'd rather have a day of major stress than a week of building stress."

"I can't be bothered."

You know that sometimes when you put things off, it feels good. You know that you let yourself do it. Know the real reason. Be honest with the person who matters most – you. You don't have to tell anyone else, but you deserve to know.

3. Take steps to destroy procrastination. Analyze your reasons for putting things off.

"I do my best work last minute and under pressure!"
Do you really believe that you can only do great things because you're forced to?

"I like to keep stress to a minimum by leaving things. I'd rather have a day of major stress than a week of building stress."
Do you really avoid stress during that week? Are you sure it doesn't niggle at you, make your stomach churn as you drift off to sleep at night?

"I can't be bothered."
Cool, do you want you sleep instead? Play Playstation? It's your life. And if you really want nothing more than to live at home until you're 35, clock Spyro, and make a you-sized dent in your bed, do it. But think about the stories you'll tell when you're old. Think about looking back on your life... Do you want to say you had a dream, and couldn't be bothered? Or do you want to grin, and know that you went out kicked some serious ass?

Here's the truth: you've been kidding yourself. Your tricky brain wants you to put things off because it feels safer. If you don't try hard, you won't get hurt, right? No one can tell you that you suck, if you don't give it your best shot. It's time to change that. Be brave and give it your all, no matter what. Do your best work and feel proud, not because it's last minute, but because it really is your best work.

4. Keep it up. Remember, you don't have to be a superhero all the time. But when a project is due, or something needs your attention, throw on your cape and go hard!

Ending procrastination means digging deep, looking for the reasons you do things. It means finding out what's in it for you. What do you get out of leaving things until the last minute? And when you uncover your reasons, pull them apart. Decide that if anyone's going to trick your brain, it's going to be you! Imagine! You can decide what's important to you. You can take your power back! Doing this might seem like hard work, you might even want to put it off! But it will make a big difference to your world.

Delay Procrastination Now!

Go through your blueprint. Next to the steps that aren't complete, ask yourself:

1. Am I putting this off?
2. Why? (No really, why?)
3. How do I feel when I put it off?
4. How would I feel if I jumped in today? What do I really want? Feel the power of being able to choose. Start now! You are on the path to exactly what you want!

Okay, so maybe you don't put things off. Maybe you don't even get started. Have you ever felt like that? Just plain lazy. You shrug. You stop caring. You tell yourself, "If it's meant to happen it will," or "It's so good to watch TV." Being lazy can feel great, but like procrastination, kills the one thing you can't get back: time. Your days are limited. Your minutes are precious. Taking action this second brings you closer to your dreams, and doing nothing pushes them further away.

Luckily, your brain has a function that shorts-out laziness. Motivation. When you are motivated, you are excited, determined, and ambitious. You want to make the most of your time and your life! Motivation is a massive power at your command. Find yours! It's your juice, your drive! Figure out what makes you want to get up, go out, and kick ass!

There are two main ways to motivate yourself. You can aim for what you do want, or avoid what you don't want. Here's the difference:

- Bex studies hard because she doesn't want to ever be unemployed.
- Lily studies hard so she can be a qualified crime scene investigator.

- Eltham saves up so he doesn't have to borrow money.
- Tobias saves up so he can travel to Asia.

Can you feel it? Both kinds of motivation can work, but one of them feels more positive, more exciting. When you move towards something, it opens up your heart. It puts fireworks in your future, and tingling in your toes. And for your blueprint? You can feel good about moving towards your perfect world, plus you can feel good about every step along the way.

Here's the trick: slot motivation into your blueprint. Add it in for every step, every level, and every achievement. What kind of motivation? Whatever works for you! Let's look at some ideas:

Rewards! What makes you feel happy? Music, presents, petting baby animals, watching your city, time at the beach, hot chocolate…

Recognition! Praise, awards, certificates. Find out how you can achieve official recognition for your goal, then sign up! When you get certificates, frame them. When you get awards, display them. Tell the universe you want more! Is it praise you're after? Recruit a friend, a parent, a sibling or an online partner. Ask them to check with you every day, and praise you if you're achieving your goal. Don't be embarrassed to ask for what you want. Put yourself first! What's sillier: to make a goal and give up, or to ask for help, and get what you want?

The future! See yourself taking over the world! Daydream, imagine, marinate. Just thinking about your perfect world can be enough. It's much easier to do something hard, when you know that it leads directly to the world you want!

Achievement! Keep your goals where you can see them. Check off your blueprint, and giggle as you achieve each one. Look at the goal list, admire yourself for planning domination of your world, and enjoy how far you've come.

When you take action you make a difference to the world. Every email, phone call, workshop, study session, kind thought, big smile. Find out how you can want to take

that action. That's the button. That's the drive. Find it –
now!

Motivation

1. Make a list of things that motivate you.

2. Add motivation into the steps of your blueprint. Small
rewards for small actions, building up. Now you're not just
working towards long term goals, but short term rewards!
Need some more ideas? How about: music, movies, time
with friends, being outside, shopping, writing, food, playing
with pets, gaming, napping... Whatever makes you happy!

World domination is a big deal, and it's okay to be
nervous! Life can be scary. It can be stressful. You may
have heard that a little bit of stress is good. Adrenalin
pumping before the big test. Sweaty hands walking up to
the podium. Stress can give you an edge. But it can also
really hurt you. Headaches, insomnia, stomach knots, and a
racing brain can all be signs that it's time to look after
yourself. It sounds weird, but you should spend some time
every day doing nothing. (Weird, because didn't we just
decide laziness kills time? And now we're going to
schedule in nothing time? But there is a difference between
being lazy, and getting recharged. And you'll know it
because when you're being lazy, part of you feels guilty,
and then all of you feels stressed. Meanwhile, recharging
can make you even more productive!)

Real relaxation isn't lazy. It eases your racing brain. It
gives you a sense of peace, and a boost to power on!

Choosing to do nothing gives your mind time to settle and absorb new wisdom. Your body is magical; it uses peaceful time to rejuvenate. Relaxation makes your eyes shiny, and your fingernails strong. Really! So sit quietly, listen to music, be with yourself. Take time to remember that this is your life, and you choose it every step. If you do it before bed you'll sleep better. And if you do it in the morning, you'll feel happier for the day.

Relax

List three ways you can relax for a few minutes every day. Here are some ideas: study meditation, learn yoga, read, write, take a walk, or watch the stars.

You can use this book to explore different ways to learn, grow and push your boundaries, but maybe only some of the ways will work for you. Remember: there is no one way to get what you want. There are millions of ways! So don't use tools or resources that don't feel right, just love knowing how many options you have, and that the choice is always yours!

Maybe you hate studying books, but love to talk to people. Maybe you find it hard to learn hands-on, but can learn a lot from watching others. Knowing how you learn best can make your life a whole lot easier. Once you figure it out, inject it into your world. There are degrees for book-learners, apprenticeships for hands-on; there is a perfect world for everyone. You were born to discover yours! Do what feels right to you!

The point of this scene is to open your mind. Learning is an adventure. One that you're part of your whole life. Take your time, be curious. If something grabs your attention, follow it through. If it looks interesting, find out more. You don't have to be the best at everything, but you can be the best at understanding you! Don't you want to know why you get mad, or why you can't stop smiling? Don't you want to know why sometimes your heart aches, and you don't know what for?

Focusing in on your passions doesn't have to be quick, and might not always be easy. But learning makes failure impossible! Because if your goal is to learn, you can make the best out of every situation. There are so many choices, so many options. And it can be incredibly frustrating if all you do is come up against subjects, projects, people and ideas that rub you the wrong way. Luckily, you can be sure that figuring out what you don't want, is just as important as knowing what you do! So embrace and hunt down every opportunity to learn. Not just through your own experience, but by listening to people, reading books and watching TV or movies (the experiences of others). You don't have to know everything. But every time you knock out an area of life that is so-so for you, you're another step closer. You can be just as proud of saying, "I don't want to be a nurse, a chef or work with numbers," as saying, "I want to be a teacher."

The most important things you'll ever learn will be about you, they will make your life smoother, easier, and more fun. Knowing yourself lets you develop your world, and tweak it to fit you perfectly. Start now!

Learn

What motivates you?

How can you relax each day?

*When your goal is to learn, you can
make the best out of every situation.
If something is getting in the way of
what you want, it's time to take charge!*

* * * * *

Scene 6: Expose Yourself

"Be bold and mighty forces will come to your aid."
Basil King

* * * * *

What if the one thing that you're on this planet to do, is the one thing you won't try? Fear can eat at your oomph. It can get in the way of the things you want, and it can suck away your power. I read that if you're not afraid, it's not brave. So, the idea here is not to stop feeling fear, because you won't win that bet. We're not going to zap your fear away; it's part of the deal. Fear can show you what you don't want, fear can help you decide, and fear can guide you when nothing else can. So, let's find a way to make fear work for you. Because if there's one thing you need to dominate your world, it's oomph - and plenty of it!

(During this scene, watch out for your brain trying to snuggle up to smugness. Maybe your brain says, "I'm not afraid of anything!" So instead, it uses a different word – do you hate math? Is it because it's not easy for you? Your brain can be naughty and might try to trick you, saying you hate math, rather than admitting you are afraid of failing or seeming stupid. And if that makes you feel better, great. But if you want to do something about it, then let's trick your brain right back! Make this section "Things I Hate." Life isn't about being right; it's about finding your way and feeling good while you do it!)

Now, like you did with your world, and your powers, the first thing to do here is define your fears. Get right up close and scary. What makes your skin crawl? Your guts churn? Is it spiders? Paper cuts? Public speaking? Let's check out the different kinds of fear: brain fear, heart fear, and kryptonite.

Fear and hate can be things that our brain creates. We have a bad experience: a spider jumps out, a teacher embarrasses us, we nearly drown, or we eat too much cotton candy. Our brain takes that one experience and blows it up, makes it huge. Suddenly we are scared of all spiders, we can't speak up in class, or we won't go near the water (or the circus). But guess what? We can take on our brain fears – because we are in charge of the brain that creates them!

But what if the fear is in our heart? What if we are afraid of a person or a situation? What if we fear for our life? Sometimes fear lets you know that you're on the wrong path. It's a sign that says, "Go a different way," or "This isn't safe for you." Sometimes freeing yourself from fear means moving away from something. Away from a person, a place, or a situation. When your heart feels fear you are allowed to run. You should run. Trust yourself. Get help.

Everyone deserves to feel safe in their world, especially you.

Or what if your biggest challenge in life is something you can't change? Something about your brain, your body, or your family that's out of your control? Like Superman. Even with all of his superhuman strength, one lick of the element kryptonite, and Superman's powers are gone. Luckily, Superman knows this. He's figured out that he probably shouldn't hang out in kryptonite malls, or wear kryptonite pajamas. But imagine if Superman didn't know about his kryptonite issue - he could be out shopping and not know what hit him. Same for you. You have your powers, but you have your challenges, too. The trick is to know what they are!

Brain fears, heart fears, and kryptonite. Now that we know the difference, let's get to you! Start with brain fear. Begin thinking about how brain fears might affect your blueprint. Are you afraid of being alone? Afraid of failure? Afraid of having no money? Or are you worried about what people think of you? No one else needs to know, so be honest.

Look at your list. Then make a decision. Are these things bigger than you are? No way. Will they get in the way of what you want? Maybe. Do you have to overcome them all? No, not all of them. You can choose to tackle or ignore any part of your life - if you are willing to accept the consequences. One thing I can tell you, there is an incredible power that comes from taking on a challenge. From knowing that you can overcome something that seems ready to crush you.

After high school I fell in love. Quentin Tarantino's work filled me with more passion than my existing plan for a career in advertising, so I left to study film. My teachers told me not to go, they said it was a waste of time, and to focus on my academics. But I couldn't listen. I was in love.

When the course was complete, my passion was all but dead. I had gone to film school full of excitement, looking for a sense of unity. I had expected to meet people that loved movies like I did, people who wanted to change the world through storytelling. Instead, lunchtime conversations were filled with, "I am going to earn so much as a director," and "Quentin who?" My classmates were pushy, bold, and full of nous. I shrank into the background. I felt like I didn't belong there. Film school was my first heartbreak. It hurt like hell that something I wanted so much, could feel so wrong. And on top of knowing that film was wrong for me, I suddenly felt like I couldn't go back to my old life either.

I wonder now if it was bad timing, my perception of the other students, or part of something bigger, because my dreams, my blueprint, my entire life was reshaped after that. I came home from film school and had a meltdown. With my future dissolving ahead of me, I decided to change everything until something felt right. I pierced my eyebrow, bleached my hair and dyed it blue, and enrolled in a Toastmaster training course called Speechcraft. Speechcraft courses offer training in public speaking, and are designed to boost confidence. I decided that Toastmasters would be the perfect antidote to my post-film-school-depression. I'd be able to build up my CV while I figured out what I was going to do next.

The course started at 7am. Public speaking before the sun came up? Perfect. It meant people were half-awake, and hopefully wouldn't remember if I was terrible. Not that I thought I would be. I planned on going along and having some fun. Maybe even coming out with a certificate and an oomph injection.

Meeting one. The first exercise was to speak for one minute on a subject with no preparation. As soon as I was given the topic, "All the World's a Stage," I was super-confident. My brain kicked into gear, telling me, "It's an easy topic; I've got lots of ideas. I'm going to kick ass!" I stood up, big grin, confident. I turned to face my audience of eight. My brain sped up, panicky: "I'm sure it seemed like a lot less people when I was sitting down. Oh my God. Omigodomigod. Eyes. Just so many eyes. Eight heads, two eyes each. That's sixteen eyes, right? All looking at me, waiting for me, filled with expectation. And who did I think I was to say anything? To expect these eight grown up people to be interested in anything I have to say?" I opened my mouth, and all that came out was, "Oh my God oh my God." Screws weren't just loose in my head; the whole conveyer belt had come undone. My mind was spinning, and all I could get out for the entire minute was, "Oh my God." Over and over again.

The rest of the meeting was a blur. I was still panicking – what happened? Why wouldn't my thoughts sit still, and come out one at a time? Why couldn't I control my own brain? But I didn't care, because I was never going back. I would find some other way to get over film school, because I wasn't going to do it by torturing myself.

Was I freaking out? Definitely. But did I feel fear? Not until the meeting ended. Because afterwards, several people in this group of strangers felt compelled to approach me. Most of them told me, "It'll be all right." Some of them hugged me. But all of them left me with the impression that I was much, much worse than I had thought.

I left the meeting, called my mom to pick me up, then sat in the phone box and cried. I had gone along for some fun, and all I had done was find another thing I sucked at. Another thing that I wasn't cut out for. More stuff in my life that made me feel like a stranger. Suddenly I got angry. I didn't want there to be anything in this world that made me feel so powerless. I didn't want there to be anything I couldn't do. So I decided that I would go back.

I've been a Toastmaster for a few years since then, and have achieved a lot during that time. But nothing I've done has taught me more than the fear I felt at that first meeting, and knowing that I choose. I choose what scares me. I choose what I can and can't do. I get to decide exactly how I want to handle my fears.

They teach us at Toastmasters that fear is a physical response, and your body can't keep it up forever. Me? I've been scared of whales for a long time. These days I get a kind of bizarre death-defying thrill out of watching whale documentaries, and noticing how my heart pounds and my hands sweat. Because I know that my body can't keep it up, so little by little I'm building up my "whale resistance," and one day I'll be able to look at one without thinking I'm going to die. Public speaking, people, whales: I can come up with ways to overcome my fears, and so can you!

Fears / Hates

1. List the fears / hates you have for each part of your blueprint. Awareness is the first step to dissolving fear.

2. The next step is deciding what to do! Look at the list. Some fears you might decide to attack full-on, some you might let yourself have, and some you might try to work on over time. Figure out which is which! Attack or accept?

3. Decide whether you want to tackle any of them. You don't have to!

4. Start creating strategies. What kind of strategies? Whatever works for you! Maybe you will full-on face your fears. When you make your fear something that you do deliberately and regularly, you can full-on face your fear and dissolve its power over you. For example:

- Scared of public speaking? Join Toastmasters.
- Hate math? Join the Mathletes.
- Scared of spiders? Get a pet one! Or (less extreme but just as effective), get the biggest, creepiest, hairiest picture of a spider you can. Post it up somewhere you can see it, and smile at the picture every day. It will get easier!

If full-on is a little fast for you, try it bit by bit. Study yourself, and notice what happens to you physically when you are afraid. What thoughts race through your mind? No one knows you better than you. See if you can change your thoughts. Why not? They're your thoughts to change! For example:

- Afraid of failure? Decide that if your goal is to try, you will always win!

- Afraid of rejection? Start seeing every "no" as one step closer to the inevitable "yes" that's on its way!

- Hate not fitting in? Know that you are special because you don't fit in!

When the fear is in our brain we can go after it, train it, and control it to change our world. But what about when the fear is in our heart?

When fear is making you do things that don't feel right, or say yes when your heart says no, find someone to talk to. Go to a parent, a teacher or a counselor. Send an anonymous email. Keep going until someone hears you. Sometimes asking for help or walking away can be just as hard, and just as strong, as facing a fear.

Kryptonite is totally out of Superman's control. It's not something he can "work on." He can't just, "get hard," or "snap out of it." Kryptonite is part of Superman's life, and his best option is to accept it, and figure out ways to keep interference to a minimum. There are things in your world that no matter how much you dislike them, are here to stay. No amount of planning will "fix" your diabetes, your short sightedness, or your dyslexia. The key is to accept these things as part of your world, and look for ways to integrate them. And you know what? There may even be ways to turn them into strengths! Let's go: what's your kryptonite?

Kryptonite

Your kryptonite is part of who you are. Can you see how your challenges might be secret strengths? For example:
- Your shyness means you are observant.
- Your broken family makes you more sensitive to others.

- Your autism brings out your creativity.

Remember: kryptonite can be a secret strength. Don't be afraid of not being perfect, it might be what makes you amazing!

If you want to make a massive change, and take on your kryptonite, get help! Want to ease your diabetes? Speak with your doctor. Considering laser eye surgery? Talk to your optometrist. Check in with your friends or get your parents on board. Just because you're doing it for you, doesn't mean you have to do it alone!

Everyone fears or dislikes things, everyone has challenges. But not everyone faces them. You could go your whole life, and never speak your truth, stand up for yourself, or hold a spider. Or you could be a superhero, someone who goes out and kicks ass. Someone who does it in spite of the fear. You know what? Some of the bravest people I know do things with their brown pants on. It's okay to fake it and, unless you tell, no one will ever know. If you're not afraid, it's not brave. Be honest about your challenges, and know that you can choose. You can do something about your fears as easily as you can take over the world: one step at a time – starting now.

The greatest super power is knowing yourself, and using your powers to create the world that you want. Prepare, be brave and expose yourself!

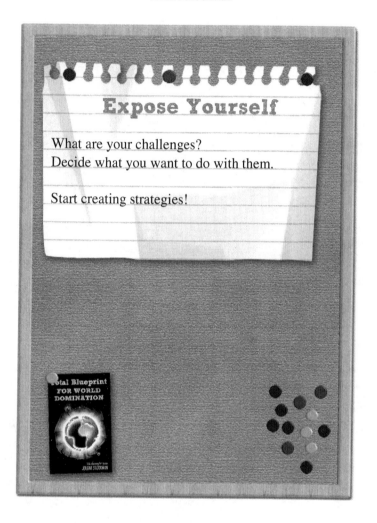

Expose Yourself

What are your challenges?
Decide what you want to do with them.

Start creating strategies!

Don't be afraid of not being perfect,
it might be what makes you amazing!

You can do something about your fears as easily as you
can take over the world: one step at a time – starting now.

* * * * *

Scene 7: Get to the Yes

Ka mate käinga tahi, ka ora käinga rua.
"There is more than one way to achieve an objective."

* * * * *

There's only one person in the world that you have complete control over. Everyone else has their own world to dominate, their own blueprint they're working to. But just because you're only in control of one person, it doesn't have to mean you're on your own. You can build an army that will work with you, and make your world smoother, easier, and all the more possible!

Here are two good reasons to start recruiting an army. One: good people make you feel good! They smile, inspire you, laugh at your jokes, bail you out, or talk you through. Two: having cool people with know-how on-call saves time. Two heads aren't better than one, but two brains are. If you're going to take over the world, you'll need people;

for connections, advice, moments and milestones. And of course, success is more fun if you have people to share it with!

Get ready. Your army starts with you! You are the leader. You set the example, and you lead the way. You decide who you want on your team and as part of your world. And you know what? You already have an army! You probably just don't call it that.

Your friends, family, advisors, role models - they are your army! Your army is made up of the people who give you what you need. It can be hundreds of online followers, or one inspiring friend. It can be a character, a celebrity, or a close-knit family. Whatever works for you! Think about your world, are there people in your life right now that inspire or support you?

Your Army

1. Who is in your army right now? Friends? Family? Teachers? Counselors? A boss? Characters in a book? Your online followers? A movie star?

2. How do these people support your world? Do they inspire you, give you advice, praise you, keep you on track, or something else?

3. You may like to collect photos or images of these people. Admire your army. Know that you are supported in your world. Let their names or pictures show you that you can do anything.

Right now, in your town, there are people making their dreams come true, people having fun, working smart, and living their dreams. You may shop at their store, or walk past their construction site, you might read about them in the paper, or hear about awards that they've won. Start thinking: is there anyone else you want to include in your army? Go out, hunt around. And always, always look for people who love what they do. You can learn more from the waiter who treats the customers as family, than the restaurant owner who dreads coming in to work. Job title means nothing, attitude is everything.

The whole world is at your fingertips. Real, imagined, and online! All around you, there are people who are where you want to go, people with strengths you can learn from. If you have a question, there's an answer – your army is everywhere!

Once you identify someone, kick into gear! Talk to them, email, tell them they have a skill you admire, tell them you want to know their secret. This will not only make them feel great, (imagine if someone asked you!) but their response may be a jewel that you use for the rest of your life. Enthusiasm is infectious – give it to everyone you meet! Let people know that you're super-keen, get in their faces with your talents and your needs. When you ask for help, the universe opens up.

When I was eight or so, I wanted to work at the donut caravan in the mall. I loved the sugar-coated sugariness of donuts. I believed nothing would be better than a job where I could spend my days breathing in that smell. One day I got brave and asked the donut lady if I could have a job. What she said changed me. She said, "I want you to come back and see me when you're twelve." I was so happy, as far as I was concerned, I had a job! I just had to get a little older. It didn't occur to me until years later that she was probably fobbing me off, but her positive reinforcement of my action changed me. She taught me to get to the yes. She hadn't said no. She had said, "Yes, when…"

"No" takes options away, "yes, when" gives you a choice. You can choose to create the "when" that is required (when you're older, when you get your license, when you learn Italian), or choose not to accept the terms. Look for a way to get the yes. There is always a way. Shrug off the no's – they are temporary. This is your world. In your world there is only yes. It won't always be without conditions, but you will always have a choice.

Getting to the yes can mean different things: it can mean getting the love, getting the job, or just getting in the door. Your "yes" might come from a parent or friend, an employer or a receptionist. Your "yes" could bring you one step closer, or it could land you smack-bang in the place you've been dreaming of. It doesn't matter who, what, when, or why - getting to the yes is up to you!

When you're fourteen and looking to take over the world the last thing you want to hear is, "You don't have enough experience." Building an army reminds you that even though there are plenty of people who'll tell you that you can't, there are also a whole heap who will tell you that you can. Know that there are hundreds of ways around everything. And everything is possible for you! You can study, you can learn on the job, you can build an army, and you can take over the world. Whether you're twelve, twenty, or one hundred and two; you can start absolutely anything, right now!

It's time to expect success, and get to the yes! Here are some ideas:

Volunteer: Join groups that will involve you with a range of people, or support causes that interest you. Learn about organizations in your community that make a difference. You'll find that the most interesting people usually have the craziest schedules. And people who are willing to give their time and gifts to help others are respected for it. They often have connections that can support your mission, and qualities that you can absorb. Plus, there's that cool way the universe tends to look after people who care about others!

Experiment: Try everything! What's it like to work with animals? With kids? In an office? Scooping ice cream? Work experience is win-win; the companies get an enthusiastic team member, and you get to try out every possible world! (Hey, and if you don't know what you want to do, this is a great way to start knocking out what you don't!)

Read: Find inspiration and motivation in the stories of others. Read about people who have the lives that you dream of, analyze their success, learn from their mistakes. Reading lets you figure out how to overcome obstacles and handle criticism, before you have to go through it for real!

Get to the Yes

1. Look for people or organizations that match the different areas of your blueprint. For example:
- Want to work with animals? Check out a vet, the zoo, or the RSPCA.

- Want to get into publishing? Find a local writer, go to the library, or jump online.

2. Does anything spark a special interest for you?

3. Make contact! Ask questions, learn more!

Many of the people and places you've identified will be more than happy for you to go in and check out what they do. There may even be opportunities for interning, life experience, or who knows what! And remember, there's always more than one way to shell a jelly bean! The first business says no? Try another, then another. You can't make anyone do anything, but you can knock on doors until the right one opens.

Persistence can be a powerful tool. And super-persistence comes from super-desire. The passion to try for something over and over, no matter what gets thrown in your way. World domination can ignite super-desire. If you want something greater than anyone else, you'll be willing to be greater than anyone else. And persistence isn't just about trying and trying and trying again, it's about creativity, problem solving, finding alternatives, working smart, believing in yourself and believing in your goals.

You might hear, "no," "impossible," "it can't be done," and all the rest of the crap that some people want you to believe. You can't take this personally – firstly, because it distracts you from your own world, and secondly, because it's not about them. Everyone else is working on their own goals. They're not rejecting you or your ideas because it gives them some kind of crazy thrill; you are just not meeting the needs that they have at this time. How people react to you often has nothing to do with you. If they have a problem with you, your idea, your passion, the way you dress, or the way you talk, it's just that - their problem. You never know what you're walking into when you deal with people. You could go for a job interview the day the manager finalizes her divorce, or email a business when their system is down. You can only control you. So: negotiate, adapt, be creative, and be persistent. There are opportunities everywhere! You can learn something from every person and every situation when you are curious, interested, and open-minded.

When I was learning to drive, I was told, "Drive like everyone else on the road is crazy." If you do that, you can anticipate the craziness, but still stay focused on your driving. It's the same with people; you can only control how you live your life. Everyone else is on the same planet but not in the same world. Don't be thrown. Be ready for anything. Because (surprise!) there is no "real" world. Your world is real for you, like everyone else's is real for them. You decide what is acceptable in your world, what is real, what is happy. No one can tell you how the world is, because the world is defined as you go. People can tell you what they have experienced, or how it has been for them. But how the world is now? How it's going to be? These things you decide. And you do this by hunting out the people who won't try to tell you how the world is, but will help you make the one you want.

Oh, and sucky people? Lots of people straight out suck. You've probably met lots of them already, and you might even meet a whole lot more. Only one thing makes this okay. Sucky people can bring you closer to the world you want, by showing you the one you don't want.

Quick tip: appreciate good people. Do it for the big things, the little things, and especially for the things that no one else notices. Thank people on paper, in person or with presents. Everyone loves to be noticed and appreciated, and your kindness might change the world for them.

People can say no, but you don't have to hear it. They can say you can't, but you don't have to prove them right. Your world is up to you, and your army is made up of the people who help you shine. Find opportunities, and milk them for all they're worth. Build your army. Your "yes" might be the next person you talk to, the next email you send, the next door that you knock on. Push through, keep moving, drive ahead. Get to the yes!

Get to the Yes

Who is in your army right now?
Admire your army, build it!

When you ask for help, the universe opens up.

Shrug off the no's — they are temporary.
This is your world. In your world there is only yes.
Knock on doors until the right one opens.

* * * * *

Scene 8: Fire!

* * * * *

You can take action this second that will lead you directly to your dream. But that doesn't make the dream your life. Once you have world domination it dawns on you: right now is all we have. Your life is made up of each and every step on the path. Because no matter how much time we spend dreaming or planning our perfect world, our life is in this moment.

I'll show you. Go there now, to the place you're dreaming of. You're accepting your award, cashing the check, celebrating world peace, and it goes like this:

You're in. You've followed your blueprint. You've obliterated obstacles, and taken on challenges. You are sitting where you've always wanted to be. You are doing what made you giggle in the opening scene. You have achieved what you wanted, and you are ready to explode with happiness and power. This is your reality check. You make a mental list of the people who have supported you, so you can thank them. You go out and inspire people to do what you've done. You speak to groups, write letters of support, write a book (!!!) or a blog. You pave the way for others to follow. You support charities that uplift your world. You make a difference!

And then it occurs to you. You always made a difference. From the time you entered the world, to right this moment sitting in your skin. You affect the people around you. You affect the world. Everything you do, and everything you don't do. By making someone smile, changing someone's mind, kicking off a dream, or ending a relationship, you send out ripples that change the world. Have you heard of the butterfly effect? It's the idea that a small thing in one place can create a big change somewhere else. Imagine that this is true. The world is so sensitive that a butterfly flapping its wings in New Zealand can create a sun shower in Las Vegas. That you make a difference, right this second. Whether you mean to or not.

Deep down (and not so deep down) you know this. You know this because it has been true all your life. Think of all the little things that have brought you here. You remember the teacher who said you could do anything, you remember the shop assistant that gave you the toy from the register because your eyes lit up when you saw it. You remember the kind words, you remember the harsh ones. These moments were fleeting but for some reason stayed with you, they taught you about the world and the people in it. You thought they taught you about yourself.

When we're little we are the most beautiful creatures in the world, and we know it. We are tiny, perfectly formed little people. Sure, if we were any other species, we'd have our own family. Instead we spend much longer in the nest, ripening our brains for independence. And whether they mean to or not, everyone that comes into contact with us has an influence on who we might become.

Millions of people, moments, words and actions have affected your life. Do you know what that means? It means that your words and actions have affected the lives of others.

John Woods said: *"You can't not communicate. Everything you say and do, or don't say and don't do, sends a message to others."*

You cannot not communicate. When you spend time with people everything you do is absorbed, and whether people remember it consciously or not, it helps mold who they are. And when you don't spend time with the people you care about? They know you're not there. They know that you missed that birthday, that phone call, that meeting. Whether it's because you're busy, sick, working, tired, or it's the final of Survivor, it doesn't matter – you send a message.

Without words or actions you can change things. Your absence makes a difference; so your very presence is a power. How you chose to wield that power will affect your experience of life, and the experiences of those around you. And that's if you do nothing.

Now, throw in your actions, your thoughts, your responses, your intentions... You have a massive responsibility. What if we are so much more important than we realize?

Marianne Williamson said: *"Our deepest fear is not that we are inadequate. Our deepest fear is that we are powerful beyond measure. It is our light, not our darkness that most frightens us."*

What if this is absolutely true? What if every one of us is mind-blowingly, world-change-ingly powerful? If you knew that, would it make a difference? Ask yourself this question. And wait for the answer. Listen to the part of you that is made of the same stuff as stars. The same stuff as Shakespeare. That part knows for sure that you are special, that your life has a purpose greater than anything you can imagine. That's the only part worth listening to.

To me the question is; what makes me happier – believing that I was born special or believing that I don't make a difference? Hey, there's evidence for both. But only one makes me feel good. And it's the "what if" that pushes me to be bigger than myself. Because what if, like Superman, everyone is born with powers to discover and grow into? And what if, like Batman, everyone has resources to uncover and utilize?

When we become the superhero we were born to be, our world is shaped around us. We also change the worlds of the people in our lives.

If someone speaks to me harshly, I can't focus on anything else until it's sorted. If you knew that your tone could set me worrying for the weekend, would you still do it? Or what if you knew that your sweetness could have me bouncing off the ceiling for a week? Would it make a difference?

You can make people feel good with a smile or a thoughtful gesture. You have that infinite power. Holding the door for someone can change their day, kind words can change their life. I find it hard to accept praise, but when something gets through I treasure it like a jewel. I admire it, tuck it away, and bring it out when I feel dark. If I think I can give that gift to someone else, I don't hesitate. I make a difference, and I know that because you make a difference to me.

Millions of Moments

1. Think of the moments in your life when other people have helped you to feel really good. Happy, connected, loved, excited. Think of big moments and little ones. They all count!

2. Notice how good you feel just remembering them. If you can't think of any, try imagine some – your brain won't know the difference! An imagined kiss can feel as good as a real one!

3. Find ways to make other people feel good. Big and little.

Time flies. And you will change the world. Not because of what you do for a job, or how much you earn, but because in all the time you exist there will be millions of moments where you send messages. With what you say and don't, with what you do and don't.

Once you are dominating your world the things you do are magnified. Do things that make you proud. And do things that make the world better. But know that you change the world in every moment.

When you send kindness out, it comes back to you. It ripples and multiplies. It grows, it bounces back. This is how you change the world. Little by little, big by big, starting now! Don't wait to be rich or famous or anything else change the planet. You're doing it now.

Your blueprint so far is a plan to create your perfect world. Let's go deeper. Because while your goals describe what you want and where you're going; your intentions take you to the next level! Your intentions are heartfelt, they explore how you will do things: how you will feel, how you will act. This is the way to bring power and magic to every moment.

Up, Up and Away!
Your Intentions

1. Take each blueprint section, and write out your intentions. For you, for the people you love, for the world!

2. Make intentions part of your life:
- Intend to have a sound sleep.
- Intend to have a productive study session.
- Intend to listen carefully to your friend.

Here are some meatier examples:

- Relationships: I will create win-win relationships by being true to myself, and appreciating others. I will learn about myself through my relationships.

- Spiritual: Growing every day, I will learn to speak my truth. I will hold myself with awareness. I will develop integrity, and inner strength. I will find out who I really am.

- Health: I will build a strong body and mind from the inside out. I will fill myself with happy food, and positive thoughts. I will love the process!

- Abundance: I will create abundance in my life by contributing to the world. By giving, not taking.

- Love: I will create love in my world by giving love, and by appreciating the love that is given to me.

- Success: I will succeed in my career by learning everything I can, and looking for ways to make things better.

Your intentions are like your personal vision, they are just for you. So when you write them, be honest, kind, and true.

The fact that you exist gives you amazing power. You make a difference. Right now. In every moment that you breathe. In every moment that you live. You can't control what is absorbed, what is remembered, or what is appreciated, but you can control what you put out. You can spread bubbles, fizz and oomph in any moment. You can change the world.

The fact that you exist gives you amazing power.
You make a difference. Right now.
Spread bubbles, oomph, and fizz!

* * * * *

Scene 9: Let Go

* * * * *

You now have a Total Blueprint for World Domination. A plan that is utterly yours, to create a world that will be perfect for you. And although it is finished for today, it's a work in progress. Because now that you have dreamed and stretched, and allowed yourself to aim for the greatest of all possible worlds, there's a new path ahead.

You have to let go of your beautiful plans, and detailed goals. Have faith that the life planned for you is greater than anything you could draw up. Now? You might follow your blueprint exactly, or sculpt it as you go, but either way you've told the universe that you want more. You want more happiness, success, peace, love, joy. You want more you! You want world domination!

You control the choices you make, the actions you take, and the life you get. And as you do it, you can support others to do the same. Look at how far you've already come:

Drive Through: You decided to kick the world's ass. You jumped into your blueprint, and prepared for domination of your world!

Super You: You set the foundation. You got inspired. You decided to ask for what you want, and to be the hero of your life story. You chose to put on your cape and your red shirt. (And sometimes, your brown pants!)

World Domination: You started hunting down your dreams. You identified the things that make your heart pound, and you found ways to pull them into your life. You defined and designed the ultimate life for you.

Target: You created SMART goals to set your heart pumping. You lined up your perfect world, knowing that everything is possible!

Aim: You got it on paper. Step by step. Bit by bit. You carved out a direct path to your dreams. You created a plan – and got ready to launch!

Learn: You looked for ways to learn about yourself and your world. You decided that if learning's your goal, you will always succeed. You found out that when you ask for help, the universe opens up!

Expose Yourself: You identified your challenges. You started digging for more of the truth about you. You uncovered more ways to take charge of your world. What if the one thing you're on this planet to do, is the one thing you won't try?

Get to the Yes: You recruited an army for world domination. You found support, advice and people to share your success with. You learned that super-persistence comes from super-desire, because in your world there is only yes!

Fire: As you follow through on your plans, you now know that everything you do makes a difference to the world. You don't have to be rich or famous (or anything else!) to transform the planet. You're doing it now.

Splashed across your blueprint are your pounding heart and glowing brain. This is the plan that you can follow for as long as it feels good to you. By pushing and challenging yourself, you have opened up to the ultimate possibilities, so it's time to relax.

Give yourself the freedom to change your mind. Be flexible. Don't get so set in your plans, that when the world offers you other opportunities, you turn them away. As you go along you may discover different worlds, or open up new dreams. People leave medical school to become monks; they swap scholarships for gap years... People give up an old dream for a new one. That's your choice as ruler of your world. Your happy ending changes all the time – let it! You are a creator, a world builder, and you are ready for anything.

Let go: Your life is in the moment, and the time to enjoy it is now. Play, have fun, find ways to make yourself happy. This is your life, and the world is yours. Any way you want it to be.

Know that you can take action this day, this minute, this second, that will lead directly to whatever you want in your world. Now is just the beginning! You can prove it on paper, and you can kick it off today!

More than ever before we live in a world where anything is possible. Your blueprint will get you exactly what you want, and you will change the world. You have one life, one shot, and all the power to make it happen. Think big! Be you! Design and dominate: your world is ready when you are!

Let Go

You control the choices you make,
the actions you take, and the life you get.

Can you be flexible in your plans and
open to new opportunities? Can you let go?

*Your perfect world is always changing, because
you are always changing, too!*

*Play, have fun, find ways to make yourself happy.
This is your life, and the world is yours.
Any way you want it to be!*

* * * * *

Bonus:

Excerpt from Guide to the (U)niverse

by Jolene Stockman

* * * * *

You've got one set of skin, one life, one shot. You get just your lifetime to be happy, take over the world, live big and be you. And it starts now!

You are the world's best kept secret. You are the one and only, get-ready-for-it, blow their minds, hidden and perfect ingredient. You are the one that's going to take over the world. You are the one that's going to make all the difference. And you are going to do it - whether you choose to or not. (Imagine what'll happen if you choose it!)

We're going to go there. To the super-cool place at the centre of you. This is the light that radiates out. This is the part of you that glows. The part of you that is made of the same stuff as stars, the same stuff as Shakespeare. This is where the (U)niverse kicks off!

You™: What makes you different from anyone else roaming the planet? Like a soft drink, a chocolate bar, or a car company, you have a brand. Your brand shouts to the world, and it whispers. It tells everyone around you who you are, and what you stand for. It also tells you. Let's sharpen your brand, polish it up, and make it shine.

Change: You get to decide exactly who and how you want to be. If you don't like something? Change! Every move, every decision, every bit of learning so far, has brought you to now. So own it – then forget it. Stop rolling around in sticky old junk, and use your energy to get what you want.

Ordering: People. Situations. Stuff. You get what you want every time, so the trick is to know what you're asking for. When you order, you know it's on its way. No matter how small, huge, crazy, or world-changing, you can have it all!

First Steps: You've made the move. You're on your way. Deep breath. Now what? It's time to jump start the first steps. These tiny first steps can bring the big life changes you want. Explore the epic, key, and tiny ways you can get started on anything.

Certainty: The whole world is designed for you. Believe it. Even when things look the suckiest. Especially then. The trick is to find reasons to believe. Because the signs are there. Actually, they're (here, there, and) everywhere. Start asking for signs, and more importantly, figure out what a sign is for you.

Take world domination to the next level! Personal branding, being you, kicking ass, getting what you want... Are you ready to step into the (U)niverse?

Other books by Jolene Stockman:

Total Blueprint for World Domination - illustrated
Guide to the (U)niverse
The Jelly Bean Crisis

For more information, visit www.jolenestockman.com

Super You

How do you want to feel in your world?

_____

_____

_____

_____

_____

What is the metaphor for your life?

_____

_____

_____

_____

_____

What is your personal vision?

_____

_____

_____

_____

_____

What makes you Super You?

_____

_____

_____

_____

_____

World Domination

What do you love?

_____

_____

_____

_____

_____

What does your perfect world look like?

_____

_____

_____

_____

_____

_____

Do a Brain Dig!
Define and design the ultimate life for you.

_____

_____

_____

_____

_____

_____

_____

_____

_____

_____

Target

What do you want for your life?

_____

_____

_____

_____

_____

What is the biggest you can dream?

_____

_____

_____

What if you could do, be or have anything?

_____

_____

_____

_____

_____

_____

_____

Set some goals that excite you!

_____

_____

_____

_____

_____

Aim

Imagine yourself in your perfect world.
Write out the steps.

_____
_____
_____
_____
_____
_____
_____
_____
_____
_____
_____

Simplify your list.

_____
_____
_____
_____
_____
_____
_____
_____
_____
_____

Learn

Why do you procrastinate?

_____

_____

_____

_____

_____

_____

What motivates you?

_____

_____

_____

_____

_____

_____

How can you relax each day?

_____

_____

_____

_____

_____

_____

Expose Yourself

What are your challenges?

_____

_____

_____

_____

_____

_____

Decide what you want to do with them.

_____

_____

_____

_____

_____

_____

Start creating strategies!

_____

_____

_____

_____

_____

_____

Get to the Yes

Who is in your army right now?

_____

_____

_____

_____

_____

_____

_____

_____

_____

_____

Admire your army, build it!
Ideas to build your army.

_____

_____

_____

_____

_____

_____

_____

_____

When you ask for help, the universe opens up.

Fire!

When have you felt the best in your life?

_____

_____

_____

_____

_____

_____

_____

When are you happy? Connected? Excited? Peaceful?

_____

_____

_____

_____

_____

_____

_____

What are your intentions?

_____

_____

_____

_____

_____

_____

_____

Let Go

You control the choices you make,
the actions you take, and the life you get.

Can you be flexible in your plans and
open to new opportunities? Can you let go?

Thank you

A Return to Love, by Marianne Williamson. Published by Harper Collins, 1996.

The Quotable Executive, edited by John Woods and published by McGraw-Hill, 2000.

Toastmasters International. Build confidence and learn communication skills. Check out the clubs and courses near you at www.toastmasters.org

Basil King, Johann Wolfgang von Goethe, Albert Einstein.

Jessica Regel for her enthusiasm and persistence, and for being my yes!

Richard Tate for his beautiful work that kicks ass, and brings blueprint to life.

And a special thank you to magical genius, perfect-Paul, Paul Quicke. He makes everything seem easy, and is proof that the universe will give you so much more than anything you can dream of.

"You've got one life, one shot, and all the power to make it happen. Get ready to dream big and live big. It's all up to you. And it starts now."

www.jolenestockman.com

Made in the USA
Lexington, KY
26 November 2015